Zac Attack!

Hanson's Little Brother

Zac Attack!

Hanson's Little Brother

by Tracey West

SCHOLASTIC INC.
New York Toronto London Auckland Sydney

Photo credits:

front cover: A.P.R.F./Shooting Star

ISBN 0-590-03488-X

12 11 10 9 8 7 6 5 4 3 2 1   8 9/9 0 1 2/0

Printed in the U.S.A.

First Scholastic printing, February 1998

Contents

Zac Attack!

Hanson's Little Brother

Zac looks up to his brothers as they sing three-part harmony.

1
Growing Up
in the Spotlight

It's the spring of 1997, and Hanson is on the road to superstardom. One stop on their journey is *The Jenny McCarthy Show* on MTV. After the group performs their smash hit "MMMBop," Jenny rushes onstage, grabs one of the brothers, and plants two big kisses on his cheek.

Which brother did the blonde beauty fall for? Was it dreamy oldest brother Isaac? Was it Taylor, the group's heartthrob? Nope. It was Zachary Walker Hanson, the youngest member of the group, who won Jenny's heart. Jenny had a Zac Attack on national TV!

To Zac's many fans, Jenny's reaction was no surprise. Since Hanson first caught the public's eye with the "MMMBop" video in May 1997, it was always Taylor who was called "the cute one." But that didn't stop fans from flipping over sweet-faced, funny Zac. Whenever Hanson appears in public, screams of "I love you, Zac!" can be heard loud and clear.

What is it about the twelve-year-old that girls go crazy for? Some say it's his puppy-dog brown eyes. Some say it's his trademark Hanson blond hair. Some like the carefree way he pounds on his drums. Others are attracted to his wacky personality.

Whatever it is, you have to agree that Zac Hanson is a natural superstar. After all, he's been practicing for it for half of his life!

By now, everyone's heard the stories about how it all began. Zac's parents, Diana and Walker Hanson, have a real love for music. When Walker's job took him from their hometown of Tulsa, Oklahoma, to Ecuador, Venezuela, and Trinidad-Tobago, the family listened to the classic rock-and-roll tapes they had brought along.

When they returned to Oklahoma, the boys were so inspired by the music that they decided to make their own. Oldest brothers Isaac and Taylor started by singing two-part harmony.

"But two-part harmony didn't really sound right," Zac has said. "So they needed a third person!"

That third person was Zac, of course. Once he started singing with his brothers, a legend was born. In 1991, the brothers performed in front of a group for the first time. It was at a party at their father's office. Little Zac was only six years old!

So at an age when most kids are scribbling in their coloring books, Zac was part of an up-and-coming music group. His mom became the group's manager. She booked the boys at events and parties. Zac studied and played with his friends like a normal kid. But he and his brothers kept on singing.

In 1995, the brothers added instruments to their act. Taylor played keyboards, Isaac played guitar, and Zac pounded away on the drums. By this time, they had written over one hundred original songs together. Soon the band was playing live. That same year, the hardworking brothers recorded a CD, *Boomerang*. The next year, they recorded a live CD, *MMMBop*. This all happened before Zac turned eleven years old!

After their live CD was released, Hanson was discovered by Mercury Records. They recorded *Middle of Nowhere* in 1996. Pretty soon the whole world would be rocking to Hanson's friendly beat.

The "MMMBop" single hit number one on the charts in May 1997. Zac was eleven-and-a-half years old. That's pretty young to have a number-one hit, but Zac isn't the youngest to ever reach that goal. The youngest performer to ever hit number one is none other than Michael Jackson. *Billboard* magazine figured out that Michael was eleven years and five months old when the Jackson 5 single "I Want You Back" reached the top. Zac missed out on the record by only one month!

By the time he was eleven, Zac Hanson had accomplished more than most people do in a lifetime. His twelfth birthday was October 22, 1997. Did Zac's ride on the road to stardom slow down? No way! In fact, some really exciting things started happening after Zac's big day:

- On November 11, the band released their third single, "I Will Come to You." The second track is a never-before released song, "Cried." *Billboard* reviewed the single and predicted it was another hit, writing, "It looks like it will be a Hanson kind of winter."
- Anyone lucky enough to be watching the *Tonight Show* on November 14 got treated to a cameo appearance by the brothers. In a comedy bit, host Jay Leno had a "flashback" to the days when he was a member of Hanson. Jay wore a long, blond wig. The brothers burst into a version of "MMMBop," but Jay complained about the singing, saying, "Zac is flat!" A smiling Zac responded,

"You're tone-deaf!" Supposedly this "fight" is what made Jay leave the group. The audience loved the bit, and all of America got to see that the boys have a great sense of humor.

• On November 18, *Tulsa, Tokyo, and the Middle of Nowhere* made its debut. The seventy-five-minute video features appearances by supermodel Cindy Crawford, weatherman Al Roker, and Weird Al Yankovic. In addition to performances of "MMMBop" and "Where's the Love," the video shows an inside look at what it's like to be on tour with the band. Zac fans are thrilled to get an up-close-and-personal glimpse of their favorite Hanson. Zac lives up to his reputation as the wacky one!

• Just in time for Thanksgiving, the band's Christmas album, *Snowed In*, hit the stores. The album, which they recorded in Europe in September, features eleven songs. The brothers cover rock-and-roll holiday hits like "Rockin' Around the Christmas Tree" and "Run Rudolph Run." They also wrote some new songs, like the slow and sweet "At Christmas" and the groovin' "Everybody Knows the Claus." Listeners who keep the CD playing after the last song is over get a special holiday surprise — a visit from little brother Mackenzie.

- Thanksgiving weekend, the boys joined ABC's popular TGIF lineup with a half-hour television special. It showed the brothers playing their hits in a variety of different scenes. What a way to kick off the holiday season!
- *Seventeen* magazine's December issue hit the stands, with the brothers taking over the cover. In the photo, Zac looks like he's staring right at you, and you only.
- As of this book's press time the band was scheduled to perform live on the *Billboard* Music Awards in early December.
- *Saturday Night Live* was scheduled to welcome Hanson on December 13 for another live performance when this book went to press. Fans probably convinced their parents to let them stay up late to catch a glimpse of Zac on TV.

Whew! The Hanson action this fall proved that the group's popularity wasn't just a spring fling. But how does Zac keep up with it all? He's got a lot of energy, and it shows. And it doesn't look like he plans on slowing down anytime soon. When an Australian TV interviewer asked where the boys thought they would be in ten years, Zac replied, "Hopefully in music!" That's good news for anyone who's ever had a Zac Attack!

"Zac's the funny one." – *Newsweek*

2
He's So Wacky!

"**T**aylor's the cute one, Zac's the funny one, and Ike's the serious one," *Newsweek* magazine reported in May 1997. If you've ever read anything about Zac, then you know that he's been called everything from funny to crazy to goofy. But the most popular word used to describe Zac is *wacky*.

What did Zac do to deserve this? Well, for one thing, his brothers think he's wacky. "His nickname is Animal, from the Muppets," Isaac told a BBC television interviewer. "He's just crazy."

But don't just take Isaac's word for it. Check out these tales of Zac gone wild. Then decide for yourself if he's really the wacky one!

• **A Rocky Start.** Zac's wild ways may have started when he was younger. Zac told *BIG!* magazine how he broke his nose: "We were firing rocks off a seesaw. We put a rock on one end and then jumped on the other — the rock would go flying across the yard. I put the rock on and then Taylor whacked the other end down and somehow it hit me in the nose. There was blood everywhere." Ouch! Poor Zac! But even a broken nose couldn't spoil Zac's cute face.

• **All Wet.** Hanson recorded *Middle of Nowhere* at the studio of popular music producers the Dust Brothers. Right outside the studio was a swimming pool. How could the boys resist? "We jumped into the Dust Brothers' pool with our clothes on!" Zac said. But the fun didn't end there. Zac played the drums on one song soaking wet! Zac also had some fun with the Dust Brothers' name on an MTV interview. "They have a very clean house!" Zac joked.

• **Practical Joker.** Zac likes to see other people soaking wet, too. "We goof off," Zac told *Smash Hits* magazine. "We like to, say, climb up on a roof and drop water bombs on people. Stuff like that." When water balloons aren't handy, Zac will use whatever's available. *Sixteen* magazine reported that Zac threw chocolate doughnut holes at *Sud-*

denly Susan's Kathy Griffith during a taping of *Fox After Breakfast.* This story's a little hard to believe, because everyone knows that Zac's a junk food nut. How could he resist eating the doughnut holes himself?

• **Wacky Wheels.** Some of Hanson's favorite hobbies are in-line skating and hanging out at the mall. Zac likes it best when they combine the two. "Sometimes we Rollerblade *in* the mall," he confessed in *Sugar.* Ike admitted that security guards kicked them out the last time they tried it!

• **Sugar Shock.** *Rolling Stone* magazine interviewed the brothers at the Chelsea Piers sports complex in New York City. During the interview, Zac ripped open a sugar packet on the table and poured it into his mouth. It wasn't long before he was yelling "I'm gonna crush your head!"

• **Pierced Dreams.** During a shopping trip on *MTV's House of Style,* the boys rode down trendy Melrose Avenue in California. Zac's mom was along for the ride, and Zac begged her to stop at a body-piercing shop they saw on the street. Diana shot down Zac's request with a look. Zac was crushed.

Maybe Mom knows best. Can you imagine Zac with a nose ring?

• **Swinging and Singing.** *Entertainment Weekly* tagged along with Zac on the Hanson tour bus. Zac swung around the inside of the bus like he was at a playground. Of course, he couldn't even do this quietly. He kept everyone entertained by singing the same song over and over again.

• **Ready for Action.** *Sixteen* magazine reported that Zac takes his Power Rangers action figures with him everywhere he goes. Zac must have a thing for these tiny toys. When the band was shooting an MTV promo in Central Park, *New York* magazine reported that Zac was playing with the MTV astronaut statue like it was an action figure.

• **Louder Is Better.** Almost every interviewer describes Zac as being LOUD. On radio interviews, it's easy to pick out Zac's voice because he's the loudest one. *Sugar* magazine wrote that he "speaks in CAPITAL LETTERS a lot." Don't be too hard on Zac. Besides Isaac and Taylor, he's got a younger brother and two younger sisters.

With such a big family, he's just trying to be heard!

• **Brother Act.** Zac isn't alone in his wacky behavior. In the fall of 1997, Hanson gave a special performance at the Beacon Theatre in New York City. *Seventeen* magazine reported that when the boys were being driven away from the theatre, a car full of fans pulled up next to them. The boys rolled down their window. "Do you have any Grey Poupon?" they joked. You can bet those girls wish they had!

It sure seems like Zac lives up to his wacky reputation. So why does Zac act this way?

It could be that he takes after his older brother Isaac. Ike, as the family calls him, is famous for imitating cartoon characters. Zac tried to explain the difference between himself and Ike to MTV's Kurt Loder.

"He's goofy funny. I'm goofy stupid," Zac said. Ike didn't agree.

"We're both goofy and we're both stupid and it's funny sometimes. Oh, God!" cried a mixed-up Zac. That's when Kurt Loder suggested that it might be time for Zac to take a nap!

Zac may take after his older brother, but he has his own theory on why he acts wacky. "I'm probably just so shy that I just act wacky to make up[for it]," Zac was quoted as saying in *BOP* magazine.

Zac? Shy? The kid they call Animal? Brother Taylor backs him up: "It's really quite amazing," Taylor told *US* magazine. "Because Zac acts crazy and wild, but he'll be like, really quiet, too."

Fans should be happy to let Zac have his quiet moments. Being wacky isn't always easy.

"If I say I'm the wacky one," he told *US* magazine, "I always have to be wacky. When I act serious, it's like, 'Why aren't you wacky? Is this a bad day for you?'"

Whether he's wacky or serious, wild or quiet, you can be sure that Zac's fans love him just the way he is.

"I think everybody's tired of being sad." – Zac Hanson, *USA Weekend*

3
Love Songs
and Aliens

Of course, Zac Hanson isn't famous all over the world just because he's wacky. If he weren't making some of the catchiest pop music around, he'd just be another wacky kid from Oklahoma.

Zac may have been only six years old when he started making music with his brothers, but he's always been a part of the songwriting process.

"Sometimes, one of us will write a little bit, then the rest will add their input," Zac told *Teen Dream.* "Other times just one of us may write an entire song, or all three of us will write an entire song together. It's a spontaneous process."

Zac talks about songwriting like it's easy, but he's had a lot of practice. The brothers wrote over one hundred songs together when they were first performing.

"All you can do is just make your music the best you can make your music," Zac told *USA Weekend.*

What drives their friendly, upbeat sound? Zac still remembers the classic rock-and-roll tapes the family listened to when Walker Hanson was stationed overseas. They listened to acts from the 1950s and 1960s like Chuck Berry and the Beach Boys. "That is the best music!" Zac told *People* magazine.

The band thinks the world is ready for this kind of music again. "I think everybody's tired of being sad," Zac told *USA Weekend.* "There's still alternative [music], but some people want to listen to music that isn't so, 'I hate life.'"

Anyone who's listened to *Middle of Nowhere* can tell that the Hanson boys really have a love for life. The happiness comes through loud and clear.

All three brothers make their mark on this upbeat album. But Zac fans will probably be most interested in two songs: "Lucy" and "Man from Milwaukee" (garage mix).

"Lucy" is the only time Zac sings lead vocals on the album. Taylor explained in *Rolling Stone* magazine that the Lucy of the song is the famous Peanuts character. As Zac is singing, he is Schroeder.

"You know how Schroeder's like, 'Lucy, get off of me?'" Zac said. "I'm doing the part of

Schroeder. And how he's saying, 'Lucy, get off my back,' and he regrets it, and, in the end, he really liked her."

It's easy to tell Zac's sweet voice apart from his brothers. And when Zac sings, "Now it's done, and it's over, and I am all alone," it's enough to make you cry!

After you're done listening to that sad love song, you can flip to the bonus CD track to listen to "Man from Milwaukee." It's probably the weirdest song on the whole CD. Who do you think wrote it? Zac, of course. Who else could come up with lyrics like this?

From the look on his face and the size of his
*   toes*
He comes from a place that nobody knows
Maybe I'm hallucinating, hyperventilating
Letting this big-toed man sitting here tell
*   me about the sky*

The big-toed man is an alien, and Zac writes about meeting him at a "bus stop in the middle of nowhere." Did Zac have a real-life alien encounter of his own? No. He was inspired to write the song sitting by the side of the road in Albuquerque. His family was waiting to fix their broken-down van. The song could have been called "Man from Albuquerque," but Zac thought "Milwaukee" had a better ring to it.

Zac made more contributions to the band's second album with Mercury Records, *Snowed In,* with his drumming and songwriting skills. It's easy to find Zac's sense of humor in the Hanson original "Everybody Knows the Claus," with lines like, "Here comes Santa Claus/You know he's a big man/ Don't mess with the boss."

Snowed In also gave fans a chance to listen to a different side of Zac. His sweet voice rings loud and clear on a medley of the traditional holiday carols "Silent Night," "O Holy Night," and "O Come All Ye Faithful."

From singing love songs to writing weird songs about aliens, Zac has proven that he's a twelve-year-old with a ton of musical talent. Who knows what surprises the group's future CDs will bring?

"I guess I'm a natural drummer." – Zac Hanson, *Smash Hits*

4
He's Got the Beat

Zac doesn't have the nickname "Animal," after the Muppet character, just because they're both wild and crazy. Animal, after all, is famous for playing the drums — just like Zac.

"I'm not a great drummer," Zac has said, "but everybody says I can play, so I'll take their word for it."

Whether Zac thinks he's a great drummer or not, you can't deny that Zac's energetic drumming helps keep the band's peppy beat. Musicians will tell you that the drummer is the backbone of any band. The other musicians must follow where the drummer takes them.

That can be dangerous when you're dealing with a wacky drummer like Zac! *Starlog* magazine reported that Taylor told a top teen magazine: "Zac's the drummer, so he'll go, 'I'm the drummer, I'll do whatever I want.'... So he'll speed us up, slow us down, whatever he wants to do."

So why would Taylor and Ike trust their out-of-control brother with such an important job? It sort of happened by accident. All three boys were taught how to play the keyboards when they were young. When it came time for the brothers to take up other instruments, the family bought a guitar from a pawnshop and found a set of drums in a friend's attic.

"Nobody's arms were long enough [to play the drums]," Zac tried to explain to *MTV News*.

To make a long story short, Zac was left playing the drums because his arms were long enough for it. Ike picked up the guitar, and Taylor stayed with the keyboards.

Ike told the story a little better. "The drums we had gotten from a friend were sitting in the living room and Zac looked down at them and he was like, 'Yeah, that's my instrument!'" he explained on Australian television.

Zac only practiced for a week on the borrowed drum set before playing his first gig. Ike revealed on a YTV Internet chat that Zac has had about ten drum lessons.

"I guess I'm a natural drummer," Zac told *Smash Hits*. "Although at the beginning I wasn't doing much."

Zac had a few other problems in the beginning, too. When he first started playing, the drums weren't attached to their kit. The drums would roll across the stage as Zac tried to play!

Despite a rocky start, Zac soon became comfortable behind the drums. It could be that Zac's love for drums started when he was very young — back in the days when his family lived in Trinidad-Tobago. He told *Fox After Breakfast* that he liked listening to the musical sound of the steel drums played there.

Whatever the reason, it looks like drumming is in his blood. If you watch Hanson perform, you'll see Zac's blond hair flip from side to side as he pounds away on his drums. And *Sixteen* magazine reported that Zac straps a megaphone around his neck when he plays. That way he can ask his fans to scream louder! Of course, the fans always do.

Will Zac always be keeping the beat for Hanson? Zac himself isn't sure. He told *Rolling Stone* magazine that he's got to keep an eye on younger brother Mackenzie.

"He's got the rhythm," Zac said. "I've got to watch out. He'll steal my place."

Even if little Mackie takes Zac's position as Hanson's drummer, don't worry that Zac will give up on music. "There's still a lot more to strive for," he told *USA Today,* "so many more instruments to learn, you want to learn anything you can."

With that attitude, Zac will be making music for a long time to come!

"I find it weird when fans scream at us because they want to meet us."
– Zac Hanson, *BIG!*

5
Zac Chats About Girls

Girls, girls, girls. Most eleven- or twelve-year-old boys don't spend too much time thinking about girls or dating. But when you're a superstar, you don't have much choice. The girls come to you.

The Hansons were being approached by adoring fans even before they were world famous. Girls in Tulsa, Oklahoma, would call them at home and scream "I love you!" into their answering machine. Today, girls scream "I love you!" wherever the boys go.

How does Zac feel about all the attention? He admits he didn't always think girls were the greatest. "We were writing songs about girls when we still thought girls had cooties," he told *Request*.

Zac may not think that girls have cooties anymore, but he doesn't seem to be interested in

31

dating anytime soon. On VH1, Zack told this story: "Somebody's big sister said, 'Will you go out with my little sister?' and I was like, 'I don't go out with people yet.' I said, 'I'm not gonna get married in the next five or six years.' And she goes, 'You could!'"

Always unpredictable, Zac was singing a different tune on *MTV News*. When asked what the band planned to do to celebrate their success, Zac piped up, "Get girlfriends!"

So how does Zac really feel about girls? Here's what he's had to say in his own words:

- **Kissing:** "I've never kissed a girl," Zac told *YM*. "But I do think about it. And it's not like there's just one type of girl who's right for me, because you say that and then you fall for someone who's the exact opposite of what you said."

  In *Smash Hits,* Ike and Zac were talking about what it would be like to go on a date. "It's not like you're going to make out," Ike teased.

  And when Zac was on the receiving end of those hugs and kisses from Jenny McCarthy, he suddenly became shy. "Zac wouldn't let her kiss him!" Ike told *Sugar.*

- **Too Busy to Date?** Even if Zac could figure out what to do on a date, he just wouldn't have the time. *Teen Dream* reported that Zac figured girls "wouldn't see very much of us, because we're always running off to Los Angeles or wherever to record albums, make videos, and perform." Zac told *Rolling Stone* that it would be sad for a girl to date someone who was on the road all the time.

• **On Meeting Fans:** "I find it weird when fans scream at us because they want to meet us. When we actually go over and talk to them they say nothing. They just look at us and go, 'Erm, um.' That's weird," Zac told *BIG!*

Here's some advice: If you want to make an impression on Zac when you meet him, think of what you're going to say beforehand. Write it down so you won't forget! Who knows? You just may be the one to open the key to Zac's heart.

Zac doesn't seem to be quite ready for dating yet, but don't despair. After all, he's only twelve. He's got his teen years ahead of him. Who knows how he'll feel about girls in a few years?

"What is there to fear? You just go and do it."
– Zac Hanson, *USA Weekend*

6
Young and Famous

It's May 1997. "MMMBop" is ruling the charts. Hanson is making an appearance at a New Jersey mall. They've made appearances before, but this one is different. This time, the mall is packed with 6,000 screaming fans!

Being adored by thousands of fans can be exciting, but it's a little scary, too. As the mall crowd closed in, Taylor's shirt got ripped. And poor Zac almost got crushed.

Zac was unhurt, but the episode goes to show that fame can have its downside. On a YTV Internet chat, Zac admitted that when he's tired and grumpy, facing crowds of screaming fans is no fun at all.

Besides pleasing the fans, sometimes the pressure of fame is too much to handle. *Hit Sensations* reported the rumor that Zac got sick before going onstage one time, and broke down in tears another time. Being famous isn't always easy, especially when you're just a kid.

Even so, Hanson's attitude toward fame and their fans is as upbeat as their music.

What's so great about being famous? Well, first, there's the thrill of seeing your face on television. As you might expect, there's a funny twist to the first time Zac saw himself on MTV.

"I said, 'Look at the cute girl — no, wait, it's me!'" he told *Time* magazine.

On an America Online chat, Zac said that seeing his face on television was cool. "It's awesome to look and go, 'That's me.' It's a great feeling."

There are other pluses to fame, too. Being in a band with number-one hits all over the world means that Zac gets to travel a lot, something he loves to do.

"Touring Europe is awesome," Zac told *People* magazine. "We can see all these places in real life instead of looking in a book."

Zac talked more about traveling on the AOL chat. "The best part [about being in a popular group] is the experience and getting to go to different places. We've already gotten the chance to go to Europe and Japan. We've gotten a great opportunity." In Europe, Zac loved the food in Italy, seeing the Eiffel Tower in France, and the Dom Cathedral in Germany.

And except for those times when they're feeling tired and grumpy, Zac and his brothers really enjoy meeting fans when they're on the road. They appreciate that fans take the time out to see them.

"Having fans wait hours and hours to see you; that is pretty awesome to think people would want to see you that much," Zac has said.

When the fans and the fame get too much, the Hansons can always escape to their hometown of Tulsa, Oklahoma. In a *Rolling Stone* interview, Zac happily talked about a break the family was planning. They were going to rent a house by a lake and unplug the phone. Even wild and crazy drummers need a rest once in a while.

Even with the screaming fans, the traveling, and the pressure of performing live onstage, Zac seems to have a healthy attitude about being famous. When a *USA Weekend* reporter asked if the brothers had any fears of success, Zac replied, "I mean, really, what is there to fear? You just go and do it."

If Zac's fans are lucky, he'll be doing it for a long time to come!

"How can we break up? We're brothers!" – Zac Hanson, VH1

7
Brotherly Love

Before Zac was even born, a television show called *The Partridge Family* featured a family of music-making brothers and sisters. Their last name was part of the name of the group. Their songs were peppy and upbeat. The family members liked to tease one another, but they basically got along great.

Sound like any family you know? When Hanson first became popular, many people compared them to the Partridge Family. Zac hates it when people do that, especially when they compare him to Chris Partridge, the drummer.

Zac may complain, but that doesn't change the fact that he is part of a big, musical family. In addition to Ike and Taylor, Zac has a sister Jessica, eight, a sister Avery, six, and younger brother Mackenzie, three.

With all those brothers and sisters, you'd

think there would be a lot of fighting. But the siblings get along amazingly well. In interviews, it's easy to see how well Zac gets along with Ike and Taylor. The three are always kidding around, with Zac hanging off his brothers like a little monkey.

Zac will be the first to tell you that they're more than brothers — they're friends. "They're like my best friends, only bester!" he told *Interview* magazine.

The three not only perform together, they also study together. The brothers have always been taught at home by their mom. You'd think being together at work and school would be enough, but that's not so. In their free time, the brothers hang out together, too.

Zac likes to play laser tag with Ike and Taylor, and the three will happily admit that they're crazy about Legos. They can build stuff together for hours.

Even the difference in their ages doesn't seem to matter, even though Zac is four years younger than his oldest brother, Ike. In fact, Ike and Taylor give Zac a lot of respect. On *Live With Regis and Kathie Lee,* Ike told Regis Philbin that "Zac definitely plays a very large part in the songwriting."

And when *Smash Hits* asked the older brothers if they needed to look after Zac, Taylor responded, "It usually ends up with Zac looking after us!"

Zac chimed in, "I guess I need looking after sometimes. We look after each other, but I don't need baby-sitting. I don't think of those two as older than me. I think they're eleven as well. To Tay we're all fourteen and to Ike we're all sixteen, I guess."

Of course, the Hansons wouldn't be normal if they didn't disagree sometimes. When Regis asked the brothers if they ever squabbled, Ike admitted that they used to break out in karate fights at practice. But the brothers claimed that they all get along pretty well now. As Kathie Lee Gifford pointed out, if they didn't get along, they might "screw up all that beautiful harmony!"

If the Hansons do keep getting along, they will be making beautiful harmony for a long time to come. As Zac pointed out during a VH1 interview, "How can we break up? We're brothers!"

Hanson has its own brand of style.

8
Zac in Black

It was bound to happen sooner or later. Like any pop supergroup, Hanson is judged not just on the music they make, but on their look. Luckily, the brothers don't seem to have a hard time making a good impression!

Of course, the most famous thing about their look is their long, blond hair. But next to the boys' hair, Hanson fans love to talk about what the boys are wearing. Visit any of the fan Web sites and you'll see a lot of discussion about Hanson fashion. Zac is just as fashionable as his older brothers. Read on to find out what kind of fashion statement he's been making:

- **The Basic Look.** To dress like Zac Hanson, the first thing you'll need is a baggy T-shirt. It doesn't matter if it's long- or short-sleeved, as long as it's nice and baggy!

Tight T-shirts are a Zac fashion don't. The next thing you'll need is a pair of baggy pants. Jeans are fine, but don't be afraid to wear something more exciting, like vinyl or leather. Army pants are a good bet, too. For footgear, try a pair of thick-soled black boots or suede sneakers with stripes. Wear your hair loose, but carry a rubber band in your pocket. If you're feeling calm you might want to stick your hair in a low ponytail for a change.

• **Cool Colors.** If you look through your scrapbook of Hanson photos, you might notice that Zac seems to like wearing the color black. Is it because it rhymes with his name? Is it because he likes the way it contrasts with his light hair? Maybe it's because Zac knows that wearing black is one of those fashions that never goes out of style.

In the "MMMBop" poster, Zac looks great in a short-sleeved black T-shirt with yellow vinyl pants. Another shirt you'll see Zac in is a long-sleeved black shirt with white stitching. You can also find black leather or vinyl pants and a black denim jacket in Zac's wardrobe.

Take another look at Zac's photos and you'll see he wears the color orange a lot, too. Black and orange? Hmmm. Maybe Zac has a thing for Halloween.

• **Brother to Brother.** Good fashion sense runs in the family. Ike, Taylor, and Zac all have a similar sense of style. In fact, it's rumored that Taylor and Zac share one another's clothes. If Zac and Ike were sharing clothes, that would be a *really* baggy look for Zac.

What's your favorite look for Zac? If you're like most fans, you probably don't care what Zac wears — he'd look cute in anything!

"We're always running off to Los Angeles or wherever to record albums, make videos, and perform." – Zac Hanson, *Teen Dream*

9
A Day in the Life of Zac

What's a typical day in Zac Hanson's life like? When you're a superstar, no day is really typical. There's always something to do. Here's a list of some of the things you might find Zac doing if you had the good luck to bump into him:

- **Touring.** Zac spent last summer and fall touring the world to promote Hanson's music.

- **Studying.** Just because you're a pop music sensation doesn't mean you don't have to go to school! Zac's mom Diana gives the boys lessons, even when they're on the road.

- **Making Appearances.** The brothers have made their mark on talk shows, radio shows, award shows, and variety shows all over the world.

• **Posing for Photos.** Say cheese! Zac and his brothers are often under the hot lights getting photographed for magazine covers, album covers, and posters.

• **Filming a Movie.** When this book went to press, *Entertainment Weekly* announced that a deal was made to film the boys' life story with the brothers playing themselves. The world may soon know if Zac can act.

• **Banging on the Drums.** Zac's love for music means that he's usually always making it or listening to it.

• **Snacking.** All that hard work can make Zac hungry. He has a real sweet tooth. If you bump into him during snack time, you'll probably see him eating Ding Dongs and Twinkies.

• **Hanging in the Tree House.** In their backyard in Tulsa, the boys built a tree house. Zac likes escaping from the world there.

• **Playing Laser Tag.** In many interviews, Zac says that Laser Quest is his favorite

Zac is the rhythmic force behind Hanson.

Ernie Paniccioli

Zac, Ike, and Taylor in concert at the Meadowlands in New Jersey.

Zac keeping the beat in New York City.

"I'm goofy stupid," Zac confessed to MTV reporter Kurt Loder.

Zac can always make his brothers laugh.

There's one thing Zac is always serious about—his music. Here, he concentrates before a performance.

Zac and his brothers meet the press!

At an MTV promo with the statue Zac tortured.

You can´t be camera shy if you are in the rock `n` roll business!

The Beacon Theatre in New York where Hanson shot the video for
"I Will Come to You."

"It usually ends up with Zac looking after us!"–Taylor Hanson, *Smash Hits*

Hanson raised a racket at the Arthur Ashe Kids Day at the Arthur Ashe Tennis Stadium in Flushing, New York.

Check out the megaphone strapped around Zac's neck. Did he use it to get fans to scream even louder?

Zac shows off his hip sense of style.

Zac went wacky pounding on the drums when Hanson was on the *Today Show*.

Roger Glazer

Eddie Malluk

"They're like my best friends, only bester." —Zac Hanson, *Interview*

"All you can do is just make your music the best you can." –Zac Hanson, *USA Weekend*

Ernie Paniccioli

hangout. It's a laser tag arena, and Zac loves to challenge his brothers to a game. The high-tech virtual reality game is played in a three-level maze called the Labyrinth. Inside, it's dark with fog and black lights, so finding and tagging your opponents with a laser light is no easy task. Zac plays at Laser Quest in his hometown. Luckily for him, they have forty-eight arenas all over the world, so Zac can get his laser fix when he's on the road.

• **Drawing Cartoons.** Playing the drums isn't Zac's only talent. Zac draws a cartoon called Superguys. Fans can sometimes get a glimpse of his artistic side on the official Hanson Web site (see page 83 for the Web address).

• **Admiring His Shampoo Bottle Collection.** That's right. Zac likes to collect miniature shampoo bottles.

Whew! How does Zac do it all — and still have energy left over to be wacky? No wonder his fans think he's the best!

Zac's birthday is October 22, 1985, which makes him a Libra.

10
Zac's Star Chart

Do the stars reveal anything about Zac's personality? Read on before you make up your mind. Then see what the stars have to say about you and Zac!

Zac's Birth Date: October 22, 1985
Astrological Sign: Libra
Libra Element: Air
Libra Planetary Ruler: Venus
Libra Symbol: the scales
Libra Motto: "I Balance"
Libra Colors: blue, pink
Libra Animal: brightly colored birds
Libra Gemstones: opal, rose quartz

The Libra Personality
Just because the element that rules Libra is air doesn't mean that Zac is an airhead! But it

might help to explain the way he always seems to be all over the place during interviews.

Librans are social butterflies. At a party, a Libra will flit from person to person. Because Librans are so attractive and charming, they make friends wherever they go, although not too many of those friendships will be deep or serious ones. Librans like to keep things light and easy.

The Libra motto "I Balance" means that Librans like to keep things in their lives nice and even. If a family fight breaks out, a Libra will try to smooth things over. The motto might help to explain why young Zac is able to balance the pressures of fame so well at a young age.

Along with balance, Librans like it best when things are in perfect harmony. Maybe that's why Zac makes such beautiful music with his brothers!

Librans like to fall in love. That could mean that Zac's girl-shy days won't last long.

On the flip side of Libra's pleasing personality is a tendency to be indecisive. Librans can never make up their minds! That may cause problems for Zac when he's trying to choose between a Ding Dong and a Twinkie at snack time.

Other Planets in Zac's Chart

When Zac was born, the planet Mercury was in Scorpio. Mercury is the planet of communication. Anyone born with Mercury in Scorpio is likely to have a really sharp sense of humor. Hmmm. Does that sound like Zac to you?

Venus, the planet that rules romance, was in Libra when Zac was born. People with Venus in Libra have an extra dose of charm and enjoy being in love. Some astrologers say that these people are very likely to be famous. That's certainly true in Zac's case!

You and Zac — Is It in the Stars?

Imagine, just for a second, that you were lucky enough to date Zac. What would the stars have in store for you? Look up your birthday in this chart to find out:

Aries: March 21–April 20

You're a high-energy person who would easily be able to keep up with Zac's busy schedule and wacky antics. Just watch out — you two could be likely to get in a lot of trouble together!

Taurus: April 21–May 21

You just might be the stable force Zac needs to calm down and keep his feet on the ground. But there's a good chance that he'd drive you crazy before too long.

Gemini: May 22–June 21

Zac loves to talk, talk, talk, and he could be attracted to you because you always have something interesting to say. You'd never be at a loss for words when you're around each other.

Cancer: June 22–July 23

You're as dreamy as Zac's big brown eyes, and he'd probably be drawn to you for that reason. You might be able to help him figure out what to do with his future.

Leo: July 24–August 23

Zac would like your high energy, but you might have a hard time sharing the spotlight with him. But who knows — you just might end up onstage together.

Virgo: August 24–September 23

Zac's parents might think you're a good influence on their out-of-control son. Zac would enjoy trying to make you laugh while you tried to tell him how to shape up.

Libra: September 24–October 23

You and Zac could have a perfectly balanced relationship. Zac's fame wouldn't bother you at all, because you'd each be happy doing your own thing.

Scorpio: October 24–November 22
Zac would most likely be attracted by your mysterious nature. This would be an interesting relationship, but it might be impossible for you to keep from being jealous of all his fans.

Sagittarius: November 23–December 21
You and Zac have a lot in common — you love to travel. If you and Zac were dating, you'd probably tag along on his journeys around the world.

Capricorn: December 22–January 20
Zac might turn to you for good advice about his career. He could come to depend on you as a trusted friend.

Aquarius: January 21–February 19
Curious Zac would find that you are always ready to introduce him to new ideas. You might even get him to think about his music in a way he's never thought about it before.

Pisces: February 20–March 20
You would be great for Zac's imagination. He'd recognize that you were a deep thinker, and probably ask you for help when he was writing a new song.

Other Notables Who Share Zac's Birthday

Michael Fishman: star of *Roseanne*

Annette Funicello: former Disney Mouseketeer

Jeff Goldblum: star of *Jurassic Park* and *Independence Day*

Jonathan Lipnicki: star of *Meego*

Christopher Lloyd: star of *Back to the Future* and *Angels in the Outfield*

Shelby Lynne: country singer

11
Zac Facts

If you think you know everything there is to know about Zac, think again! Some of these facts may surprise fans who think they know Zac inside and out.

GENERAL INFO

Full Name: Zachary Walker Hanson

Nicknames: Zac, Animal, Psycho, Gonzo, Prozac

Birthday: October 22, 1985

Astrological Sign: Libra

Current Residence: Tulsa, Oklahoma

Former Residences: Ecuador, Trinidad-Tobago, Venezuela

Parents: Diana and Walker Hanson

Father's Profession: Until Walker retired to work full-time with Hanson, he was a financial executive for an oil-drilling company.

Siblings: Older brothers Isaac and Taylor, younger brother Mackenzie, younger sisters Jessica and Avery

Hair: Blond

Eyes: Brown

Height: 5'3" (and still growing)

Instruments: Drums and keyboards

Drum Brand: Pearl

Useful Talents: Drawing cartoons, skateboarding

Injuries: Broke his nose while playing with his brothers

Right- or Left-Handed?: Left-handed

Toothbrush Color: Green

Known As: The "wacky" one

FAVES

Color: Blue

Food: Lasagna, hot dogs, pizza, McDonald's

Snacks: "Ding Dongs and Twinkies are my most important food group," he told *YM*.

Dessert: Lime Jell-O

Ice Cream: Chocolate

Drink: Dr Pepper

Movies: Action movies like *Total Recall* and *Twister*

Singer: Alanis Morissette

Sports: Basketball, soccer, in-line skating, skateboarding, speed hockey

Game: Laser tag

Hobbies: Building with Legos, drawing cartoons

TV Show: *Animaniacs*

Subject: Math

Toys: Power Rangers action figures

Expression: "D'oh!" (*à la* Homer Simpson)

Collection: Miniature shampoo bottles

12
Is Zac for You?
Part One

Do you think you and Zac would have a great time if you ever got together? Here's one way to find out. Imagine yourself in these situations with Zac. Then circle the answer that best describes what you would do. When you're done, check out your score to see if Zac is the one for you!

1. You're at a Hanson concert, and you wait backstage to meet Zac. Before you know what's happening, Zac is standing right in front of you. Do you:
    a) Scream, "I love you!"
    b) Say, "It's nice to meet you. I'd love to talk to you about that harmony you used on your encore."
    c) Pass out.

2. You and Zac are hanging out when Zac says, "I'm hungry!" You run into the kitchen and:
   a) Fix him a three-course meal.
   b) Say, "How can you be hungry? You just ate ten minutes ago!"
   c) Grab a couple of Twinkies out of the snack drawer.

3. Zac says, "What do you want to do this afternoon?" You say:
   a) "Let's play some laser tag."
   b) "Let's hang out and watch TV."
   c) "Let's replay your appearance on the *Rosie O'Donnell Show* over and over again."

4. You're riding with Zac in the tour bus, and he asks you to put a tape in the tape player. You choose:
   a) Weird Al Yankovic
   b) Alanis Morissette
   c) Metallica

5. Zac asks you to check out the new addition on his tree house. You say:
   a) "I'm afraid of heights!"
   b) "Last one up is a loser!"

c) "But if you climb up there, you'll mess up your new vinyl pants!"

6. You and your family win a contest and get a plane ticket to anywhere in the world. You invite Zac along, and fly to:
   a) Tulsa, Oklahoma.
   b) A quiet island in the Pacific.
   c) Italy, where you treat Zac to a delicious meal.

7. You and Zac are walking in Manhattan when you pass the famous FAO Schwarz toy store. There's a giant Lego display in the window. You both stop to look at it, when you say:
   a) "I bet we could build an awesome castle with those!"
   b) "I outgrew those things five years ago."
   c) "Playing with toys is a waste of time."

8. Zac asks you to help baby-sit his little brother. You reply:
   a) "Sure. Brothers are cool."
   b) "Couldn't we spend some time alone instead?"
   c) "Kids give me a headache."

9. You and Zac are in-line skating when Zac wipes out. He seems to be all right. You:
   a) Run to the nearest phone and call an ambulance.
   b) Suggest that you stop blading and do something else.
   c) Laugh and say, "Awesome wipeout, dude."

10. You are walking down the street when a water balloon crashes at your feet. You look up, and Zac is grinning at you. You:
   a) Storm away angrily.
   b) Yell, "I'll never speak to you again!"
   c) Grab a garden hose and give him a taste of his own medicine.

Answers
The answers that best match Zac's personality are:
1. b; 2. c; 3. a; 4. b; 5. b; 6. c; 7. a; 8. a; 9. c; 10. c

Your Score
Give yourself one point for each correct answer. Then check the chart to see if you and Zac are made for each other:

1–4 points
You and Zac probably don't have too much in common. But don't worry. After all, don't they say that opposites attract?

5–8 points

You and Zac get along pretty great, but there are still a few things that you might argue about.

9–10 points

You and Zac are a match made in heaven.

13
Is Zac for You?
Part Two

Try this old school yard trick to see how your name matches up with Zac's. The decoder will tell you what the future could have in store for the two of you. (Warning: This game is for fun only. Anyone who takes it seriously is obviously the victim of a serious Zac Attack!)

1. Write your first name across the top of a piece of paper.
2. Write Zac's first name underneath your name.
3. Write A E I O U on the third line.
4. Write 1 2 3 4 5 on the fourth line. Make sure the numbers line up directly under the letters. Look at the sample on the next page to see how to do it right.
5. Add up the number of A's in both your names. Write that number in the first column.

Then do the same with the rest of the vowels in your name.

6. Add up the numbers in the fourth and fifth lines.

7. Cross out any numbers that match. Then add the remaining numbers until you end up with a single-digit number. (If you end up with a double-digit number, add the two digits to get a single number. For example, add the two ones in eleven to get two.)

8. Look up the number in the decoder to see what the future might hold for you and Zac.

Tip: If you don't like the number you get, then try using different variations of your name. You could use your full name with Zachary Walker Hanson. Or you could try Zachary Walker, or Zachary Hanson, or Zac Hanson . . . whatever works for you.

Sample

L	A	U	R	I	E	
Z	A	C	H	A	R	Y
A	E	I	O	U		
1	2	3	4	5		
3	1	1	0	1		
X̶	3	X̶	X̶	6		

$3 + 6 = \underline{9}$

Decoder:

1. They say one is the loneliest number. You are destined to worship Zac from afar.

2. You and Zac could be a hot item for a short time.

3. Zac might smile at you across a crowded room.

4. You may marry a guy named Zac — but his last name won't be Hanson!

5. You will get seasick surfing the Net looking for live chats with Zac.

6. You might end up with one of the Hansons — but not Zac!

7. You and Zac could become good friends.

8. You will get laryngitis from screaming out Zac's name at Hanson concerts.

9. You and Zac could live happily ever after.

14
Write to Zac!

Have you been dying to write a fan letter to Zac, but don't know what to say? Use this handy format to put your thoughts on paper. Choose one of our answers or pick your own. Then use the contact list on page 83 to get your message to Zac. But remember — don't expect a personal letter or phone call in return. Zac gets too much mail for one small superstar to handle!

THE ZAC HANSON FILL-IN-THE-BLANK FAN LETTER

Dear Zac,

Hi! My name is (your biggest fan/I'm so nervous I forgot!). I live (too far away from you/in the hopes that I will someday meet you). I read that your favorite color is blue. My favorite color is (brown, like your eyes/Zac — I mean, black). So you like to listen to Alanis Morissette? I like to listen to (*Middle of Nowhere,* over and over again/the sound of your voice).

Like you, I am also a big Lego fan. If I had a million Legos, I would build (a life-sized model of you/a tree house just like yours). I also like to play laser tag. If we ever played a game together, I would (show you how the game is *really* played/let you win on purpose).

Good luck with your career! If you are ever in (your hometown), why don't you stop by and see me? We can (eat Twinkies until we pass out).

Your biggest fan,

(Your real name and address)

Where To Contact Zac Hanson
Addresses ✳ Fan Clubs
E-mail ✳ Chat Rooms
Web Pages ✳ Cyber Links

Official Hanson
Fan Club:

HITZlist
P.O. Box 703136
Tulsa, OK 74170

Record Company:

Zac Hanson
c/o Mercury Records
825 Eighth Avenue
New York, NY 10019

Hanson's Hotline: 1-918-446-3979
(Be sure to get a parent's permission!)

Official Web Page:
http://www.hansonline.com

Hanson AOL Screenname:
mmmbop@aol.com

Official E-Mail:
HITZLIST@aol.com

Other E-Mail:
hansonfans@hansonline.com

Mercury Records Hanson Web Page:
http://www.mercuryrecords.com/mercury/
    artists/hanson/hanson_homepage.html

Discography

Albums

Boomerang **(self-released)**
  "Boomerang"
  "Poison Ivy"
  "Lonely Boy"
  "Don't Accuse"
  "Rain"
  "More Than Anything"
  "The Love You Save"
  "Back to the Island"
  "More Than Anything" (reprise)

MMMBop **(self-released)**
  "Day Has Come"
  "I'll Be Thinking of You"
  "Two Tears"
  "Stories"

"River"
"Surely as the Sun"
"Something New"
"MMMBop"
"Soldier"
"Pictures"
"Incredible"
"With You in Your Dreams"
"Sometimes"
"Baby You're So Fine"
"MMMBop"

Middle of Nowhere (Mercury)
"Thinking of You"
"MMMBop"
"Weird"
"Where's the Love"
"Yearbook"
"Lucy"*
"I Will Come to You"
"A Minute Without You"
"Madeline"
"With You in Your Dreams"
"20 Empty Tracks"
"Man from Milwaukee"* (garage mix)

Snowed In (Mercury)
"Merry Christmas, Baby"
"What Christmas Means to Me"
"Little Saint Nick"

"At Christmas"
"Christmas (Baby Please Come Home)"
"Rockin' Around the Christmas Tree"
"Run Rudolph Run"
"Christmas Time"
"Everybody Knows the Claus"
"Silent Night Medley"
"White Christmas"

*a special Zac moment

Mercury Singles
"MMMBop"
"Where's the Love"
"I Will Come to You," with "Cried," a never-before-released track.

Videos
MMMBop
Where's the Love?
I Will Come to You
Thinking of You
Documentary Video
Tulsa, Tokyo, and the Middle of Nowhere